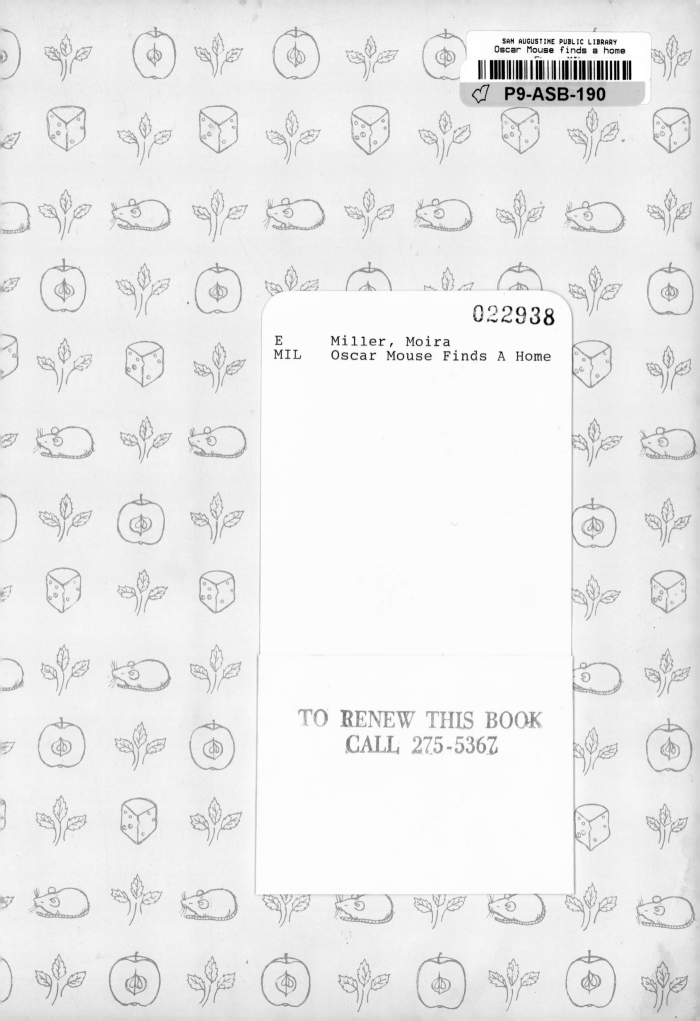

For my family
with love

First published in the United States 1985 by
Dial Books for Young Readers
A Division of E. P. Dutton
2 Park Avenue
New York, New York 10016
Published in Great Britain by Methuen Children's Books
Text copyright © 1985 by Moira Miller
Pictures copyright © 1985 by Maria Majewska
All rights reserved / Printed in Great Britain
First Edition
US
10 9 8 7 6 5 4 3 2 1

Library of Congress Cataloging in Publication Data
Miller, Moira. Oscar Mouse finds a home.
Summary: Oscar Mouse searches for a home of his own
when the attic where he lives becomes too crowded
with little brothers and sisters.
1. Children's stories, American.
[1. Mice — Fiction. 2. Dwellings — Fiction.]
I. Majewska, Maria, ill. II. Title.
PZ7.M2797Os 1985   [E]   85-1665
ISBN 0-8037-0229-9

The full-color artwork was prepared using
watercolor paints, inks, and crayons.
It was then camera-separated and reproduced
in red, blue, yellow, and black halftones.

OSCAR MOUSE FINDS A HOME

by *Moira Miller* • pictures by *Maria Majewska*

Dial Books for Young Readers • New York

Oscar Mouse lived in The Attic with lots of little brothers
and sisters. Oscar was old enough to go hunting in The
House at night by himself.

"Tell us about it, Oscar. Come on, tell us about The House!" squeaked his little brothers and sisters as they jumped up and down on him.

All Oscar wanted to do was sleep. "Quit it!" he moaned as they climbed over his bed. "And get your paws out of my ear."

But they never listened to him.

Sometimes they made so much noise that the House Cat came up to see what was going on. They were quiet then, but it lasted only until the cat had gone.

"It's no use," said Oscar. "I can't sleep. I've got to find a house of my own."

On Monday he searched the rafters and found a big pile of straw and feathers.

"Home Sweet Home," said Oscar, curling up. And soon he was fast asleep.

"Whoooooooo are you?" hooted a loud voice. "And what are you doing in my nest?" Oscar stared up at two enormous yellow eyes and a very sharp beak.

"Please," he said. "I'm looking for a new home."

"Move in with me, by all means," said the Owl, wiping traces of fur from his beak. "*Do* stay to dinner!"

"No...I don't think I'd like that!" said Oscar. Fast as a whisker he scurried through the dusty attic back to his noisy brothers and sisters.

On Tuesday Oscar found a large dark room. In the middle of the floor was a high soft bed with a cozy heap on top of it. There was no sign of an owl anywhere.

"Home Sweet Home," said Oscar, curling up. And soon he was fast asleep.

"Whazzat?" muttered the heap. It opened its huge mouth and started to snore like a train. Oscar tumbled off onto the floor, very surprised.

"No . . . I don't think I'd like this!" he said. Fast as a whisker he scurried back to his noisy brothers and sisters.

On Wednesday Oscar found a white shiny room. There were no owls and no Great Snoring Heaps. He skated along a marble shelf beside a mirror. At the end of the shelf was a soft powder puff in a round pink bowl.

"Home Sweet Home," said Oscar, curling up in the bowl.

But underneath the fluffy puff there was thick white powder that made him sneeze.

"Ah-choo, ah-choo, ah-choo!" howled Oscar. He fell out onto the shelf and sat up. Staring back at him from the mirror was a ghostly white mouse.

"Help!" squeaked Oscar. "I don't think I'd like this!" Fast as a whisker he scurried back to his noisy brothers and sisters.

On Thursday Oscar made one more try. He tiptoed downstairs.
There were no owls, no Great Snoring Heaps, no White Mice.

There was a table, some chairs, and lying on a sofa, some Very Strange Animals. They stared. Oscar stared back.

"No...I don't think—" he began, when suddenly the door opened and a pair of Feet walked in.

Fast as a whisker, Oscar wriggled in among the Very Strange Animals.

"Excuse me," he said. "Sorry about standing on your head." Then he sat very still and stared straight ahead—just like the other animals.

"Time for bed," said a voice, and one of the Very Strange
Animals was lifted up. Oscar hardly dared to breathe until
the Feet had gone, shutting the door.

"I *know* I don't like this," said Oscar firmly. He looked around for somewhere safe to spend the night. In the corner another door stood slightly open.

"Excuse me," he said, climbing down. "Oh, I'm *very* sorry." He stood on a round furry tummy.

"Squeeeeeeeeeeeeek!" said the Very Strange Animal.

"How strange!" muttered Oscar.

He slipped quick as a whisker through the open door—into a very dark cupboard.

"It smells right," said Oscar, feeling around with his whiskers.

"It sounds right," he said, listening carefully.

There were no owls, no Great Snoring Heaps, no White
Mice, no cats, no Feet, and no Very Strange Animals.

In the corner stood a large empty can labeled SUGAR. It
looked like it had been there for a very long time, although
there were still some tiny grains of sugar in the bottom.

"Yes . . . I think I like this," said Oscar, climbing over the
can and licking his whiskers. He chewed up some paper to
make a comfortable bed.

"Not bad at all," said Oscar. "I might even invite everyone down for a party. But only if they promise *not* to stay."

Oscar licked his sticky, sugary paws, closed his eyes, and curled up in his new bed.

"Home Sweet Home." He yawned and then fell fast asleep.